TOMORROW
AND
BEYOND
Masterpieces of Science Fiction Art

TOMORROW AND BEYOND

Masterpieces of Science Fiction Art

Edited by
IAN SUMMERS

WORKMAN PUBLISHING COMPANY·NEW YORK

ACKNOWLEDGMENTS

Thanks to all the editors and art directors who gave their time so freely; to Richard Gallen and Peter Workman for their patience, understanding and encouragement; to Sally Kovalchick who can't be thanked enough; to Judy-Lynn and Lester del Rey who re-introduced me to science fiction. Special thanks to Sally Bass, my un-tiring co-designer who painstakingly lived and breathed this book for six months; to Paul Thomason who functioned as art coordinator; to Vincent DiFate who was always there when I needed him. Thanks to the artists' agents, Frank and Jeff Lavaty, Lars Tiegenborn, Jerry Leff, Joe Mendola, Joseph Berenis, Harvey Kahn, Jerry Anton, Barry Friedman and David Hankins. And thanks to Ray Garissino of Italiagrafica and Jim Ahearn of Connecticut Printers who worked extra hard to assure the quality of the printing.

ISBN 0-89480-062-0
ISBN 0-89480-055-8 pbk.
LC: 78-7119

Workman Publishing Company, Inc.
1 West 39 Street
New York, New York 10018

Manufactured in the United States of America
First printing October 1978
10 9 8 7 6 5 4 3

Jacket art: David Schleinkofer
Jacket design: Sally Bass

For Rochelle, with love

CONTENTS

ALIENS ————— 18

ASTRONAUTS ————— 38

SYMBOLISM ————— 49

FANTASY ————— 80

BARBARIANS ————— 96

SPACECRAFT ————— 104

FUTUROPOLIS ————— 120

OTHER WORLDS ————— 126

SUPERNATURAL ————— 130

ROBOTS ————— 136

HUMOR ————— 140

BACK TO EARTH ————— 142

APPENDIX ————— 145

INDEX ————— 157

TOMORROW
AND
BEYOND

Tomorrow and Beyond is a rich collection of over 300 full color works of art representing the pick of the portfolios of more than 65 celebrated artists in the fields of science fiction and fantasy. The works range from the near abstractions of Richard Powers to the almost photo-real images of John Berkey; from the highly symbolic creations of Jan Sawka to the story-telling paintings of the Brothers Hildebrandt and Darrell Sweet. What all the works have in common, besides a fondness for the themes and subject matter, is a sense of exploration. They transport us to frontiers where nothing can be taken for granted; they offer us both a challenge and an invitation—a challenge to dispense with stale habits of thought, and an invitation to discover the joys of seeing the world and ourselves from a fresh perspective.

ART WITH A MISSION

Science fiction art, like science fiction itself, assumes a special mission in training the imagination. Its strength comes from its attitude towards the future: it is not afraid of technology, it is not afraid of change, it is not afraid of contemplating alternative views of reality. Some of the darker visions on the following pages are testimony to the fact that science fiction is not "mere escapism." These artists recognize the destructive potential of man's creations. Even when the themes touch on nightmare, the mood stops just short of despair. If a single lesson can be extracted from this wealth of imagery, it is that nothing conceived of by the human mind is utterly alien.

THE ALIEN

In science fiction parlance, an "alien" is a non-human creature, sometimes intelligent (or at least diabolically clever), and most likely from some other planet, time, or universe. Scientists who think seriously about such things assure us that there are millions of habitable planets scattered about our galaxy, that life almost surely has evolved on many of them, and that there is a good chance many of these life-forms have been around longer than we have, and so are quite possibly intellectually and technologically more advanced than we are. Some of us may take comfort from this scientific assurance that "we are not alone." Others may shudder at the thought that some day a superior race of beings will treat us the way human beings have treated others who have inferior technologies. For science fiction artists, either possibility is a spur to inspiration.

The paintings on page 34 show the peaceful interaction of humans and aliens. The cat-like creatures in Darrell Sweet's illustration for *Decision at Doona* are obviously intelligent; for both aliens and humans, the building of the bridge is a task requiring teamwork. It is not immediately clear who is more intelligent, but the message embodied in the composition—with the cat towering over a uniformed man who seems to be arguing a technical point—is that it does not much matter. The relationship between Sweet's flask-bearing Tyrannosaurus and the ruminative friar is equally ambiguous; if humor is a sign of intelligence, then the apparent smile of the thunder-lizard would seem to give it an edge.

The paintings of Robert Petillo and the Brothers Hildebrandt quite clearly depict scenes on planets other than earth—an odd juxtaposition of colors, some unfamiliar clothing and architecture details and we are immediately reminded that "alien" is a relative concept. Transported to a distant world by our own (or someone else's) technology, we become the aliens—with all the dangers, burdens, and opportunities that that status implies.

There was a time, a few decades ago, when the moon, Mars, and Venus were favorite locales for science fiction stories; and since astronomers could tell us *something* about those heavenly bodies—the moon had lots of craters but no air, Mars had only a little atmosphere, Venus was covered with clouds—the imaginations of writers and artists operated under certain constraints. But it is common nowadays to set a story on a made-up planet circling some distant star, since such imaginary settings are literally and figuratively beyond the reach of 20th Century science. Yet this does not mean that the creation of aliens in modern science fiction is entirely arbitrary.

In the process of inventing a planet, science fiction authors try to avoid blatant inconsistencies in matching flora and fauna to geology,

climate, etc. For example, a planet much larger than earth would have much stronger gravity at the surface than the earth does, and so one is not likely to find hollow-boned, bird-like creatures flitting around on thin legs and delicate feet. Indeed, the depiction of plausible aliens requires at least a smattering of knowledge in biology, physics, anatomy, ecology and climatology. The process works the other way as well; a glance at Brad Holland's bat-winged, ape-faced, titan-legged creature on page 20 should provide a host of clues to the nature of the world it inhabits. Vincent DiFate's regal alien with the octopoid head seems to have stepped out of Homer or Virgil; by simple manipulation of scale, the artist moves us to awe instead of terror or disgust. Ray Feibush (pages 24 and 25) uses distortions of scale for a different purpose—to create a sense of doom.

LANDSCAPE AND LIFE-FORMS

Although the "natural" landscape dominates many of these pictures, there are usually hints in the background of an advanced technology—which makes sense, of course, since none of the encounters could have taken place without some kind of space- or time-conquering machines. H.R. Van Dongen's bright-eyed, bushy-tailed centaur (page 19) seems quite at home in an artificial environment, as do the men and women depicted by Ken Barr (page 40), Paul Stinson (page 44) and John Schoenherr (page 46). But what is one to make of the disturbing figure offered by Stanislaw Fernandes (page 48)? Is this the next stage of evolution—a man made in the image of a machine?

There is no question that in some science fiction art, the machines seem more impressive, interesting, and "alive" than any so-called life forms. The spacecraft of Paul Lehr (page 109), John Berkey (pages 104 and 105) and Paul Alexander (page 121) look more like objects of worship than mere tools. Perhaps even more daunting to man's imagination than the thought of truly alien life-forms is the prospect of going out into space and encountering nothing but lifeless wastes and emptiness. Ron Miller's astronomical paintings are based on the latest scientific findings, and they look it. Scrutinizing his "Martian Highlands" and "Saturn as Seen from Rhea" (page 127), we readily concede that this is the way the camera will record such scenes some day not too far in the future. We savor in advance the technological achievement, and we thrill to the unearthly beauty—but at the same time we cannot shake the impression that these chilling vistas have no place in them for man.

SCIENCE FICTION VS. FANTASY

Most writers and artists shy away from defining the difference between science fiction and fantasy, but as good a touchstone as any for separating the two related genres is a sense of time. Science fiction concerns the future. By and large, it treats time as linear; even when a story or picture does not come with a specific date, we have no trouble believing that a calendar exists somewhere on which the events depicted can be marked off.

Fantasy, on the other hand, is essentially timeless; what happens in a fantasy story or picture could happen anytime. Since it deals with the universes within, fantasy partakes of dream-images, dream-chronology, dream-symbols. Compare the giant sharp-toothed reptile on page 34 with those delineated on page 96; the former is clearly amenable to reason, the latter can only be exorcised by heroic struggles. It seems whenever artists delve into the stuff of dreams, they are likely to bring back nightmares—as in David Schleinkofer's beast-in-the-machine (page 73), Nick Aristovulous' face-in-the-cobra's mouth (page 63) and Jan Sawka's sea-of-eyes (page 53). But there are lighter moments too, such as Robert LoGrippo's landscape *à la* Bosch (page 87).

TOMORROW AND BEYOND

This album is not a historical survey of science fiction and fantasy art. Only a few of the works date back as far as the 1950's and most were created in the last decade. Many were commissioned to be used on the covers of paperback books, the paperback industry being the largest single "patron" of science fiction and fantasy art at the present time. But there are other markets as well. Some of the art reproduced here for the first time without typographical matter originally appeared in advertisements, annual reports, sales promotion literature, or on record album covers. Some paintings were created by the artists for their own portfolios, or to satisfy a whim or expressive urge.

The backgrounds and work-habits of the artists represented are as varied as their subject matter. Jan Sawka, a native of Warsaw, lived in Paris briefly before moving to the United States in 1977. The aliens that he has conjured up (page 18) are not illustrations of anyone else's visions, but the products of his own fancy. His work, with its vivid, poster-like quality, won the International Poster Competition for 1978. Nick Aristovulous works with acrylic resins to create almost life-sized sculptures. His demented cobra (page 63) originally commissioned for a motion picture called *Sssssss,* stands four feet tall. The starkly barren photo-fantasies of Jake Rajs (pages 142 and 143) illustrate

science fiction and fantasy through photography, a very difficult task. By showing familiar objects in an unfamiliar light (as in his green New Mexican "Badlands" on page 142), he forces us to go through the aesthetic equivalent of a theatrical "double take."

There is no doubt that all the images gain depth and resonance from being seen in the company of kindred works. No artist works in a vacuum. For those who enjoy tracing artistic roots the influence of figures as diverse as Hieronymous Bosch, Salvador Dali, René Magritte, N.C. Wyeth, Maxfield Parrish, and Walt Disney can be discerned in many of these pictures. Freudian and Jungian symbols abound. Some of the more imaginative compositions might be illustrations of stories by Franz Kafka or Jorge Luis Borges. Yet there is no mistaking the freshness of the images. Whatever the constraints placed on the artist by commercial considerations, whatever the tradition in which he worked, the most important quality in selecting pictures for this collection was that the art provided a challenge to both the mind and the eye, revealed technical excellence and aesthetic qualities, presented an interesting speculative concept, and had a science fiction or fantasy point of departure. It is a strong, beautiful collection and one you are sure to enjoy.

TOMORROW
AND
BEYOND
Masterpieces of Science Fiction Art

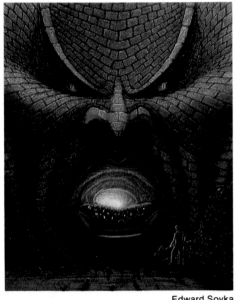

Edward Soyka

Michael Herring

Carl Lundgren

Walter Bachinsky

Brad Holland

John Gampert

Carl Lundgren

Brad Holland

Vernon Kramer

ALIENS

Jan Sawka

Jan Sawka

David Schleinkofer

David Schleinkofer

H. R. Van Dongen

ALIENS

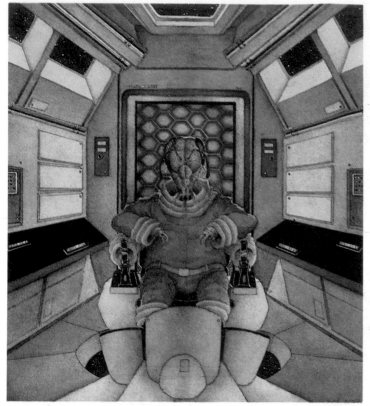

Mark Corcoran

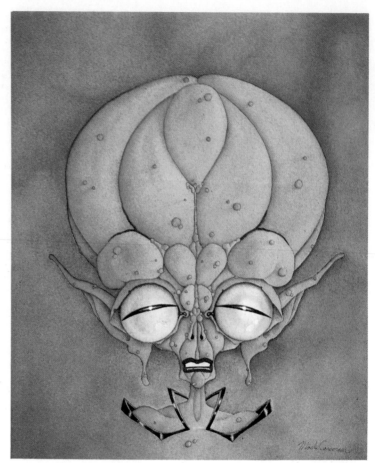

Mark Corcoran

Brad Holland

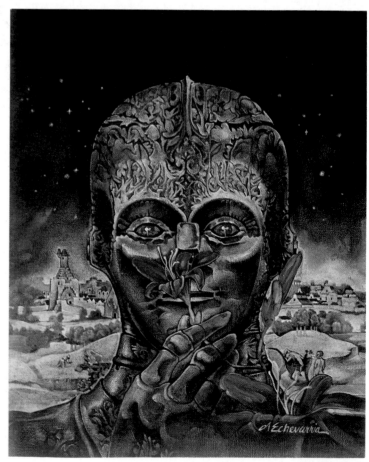

Abe Echevarria

Douglas Beekman

ALIENS

Michael Whelan

Michael Whelan

Steve Hickman

Paul Alexander

ALIENS

José Cruz

Ray Feibush

Ray Feibush

Ray Feibush

Ray Feibush

H. R. Van Dongen

Vincent DiFate

Joseph A. Smith

H. R. Van Dongen

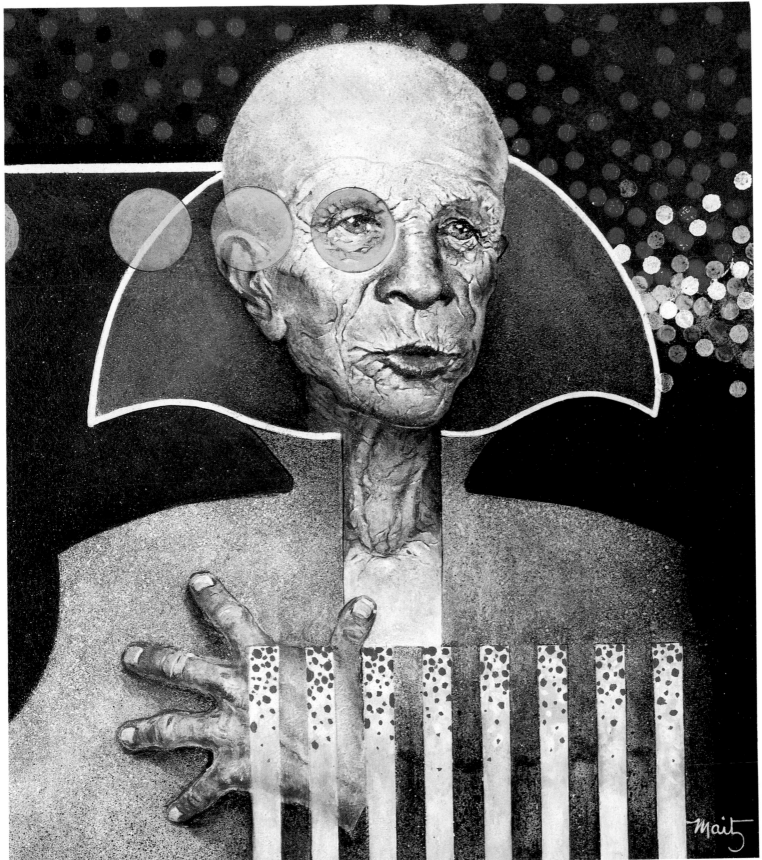

Don Maitz

ALIENS

Wilson McLean

Paul Alexander

Paul Alexander

Michael Presley

ALIENS

Wayne Barlowe

Robert Petillo

Harry Bennett

Michael Presley

Don Ivan Punchatz

ALIENS

H. R. Van Dongen

H. R. Van Dongen

H. R. Van Dongen

H. R. Van Dongen

Paul Alexander

ALIENS

Darrell Sweet

Robert Petillo

The Brothers Hildebrandt

Darrell Sweet

The Brothers Hildebrandt

ALIENS

Brad Holland

Peter Caras

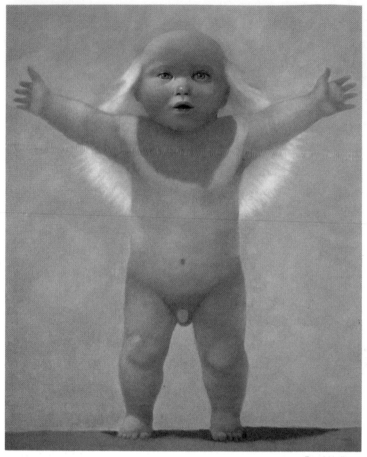

Wayne Barlowe

H. R. Van Dongen

36

John Schoenherr

John Schoenherr

ASTRONAUTS

Darrell Sweet

H. R. Van Dongen

Chris Spollen

Paul Lehr

ASTRONAUTS

Michael Whelan

Steve Hickman

Ken Barr

Ken Barr

Robert Schultz

Jan Sawka

Stanislaw Fernandes

Don Brautigam

Don Brautigam

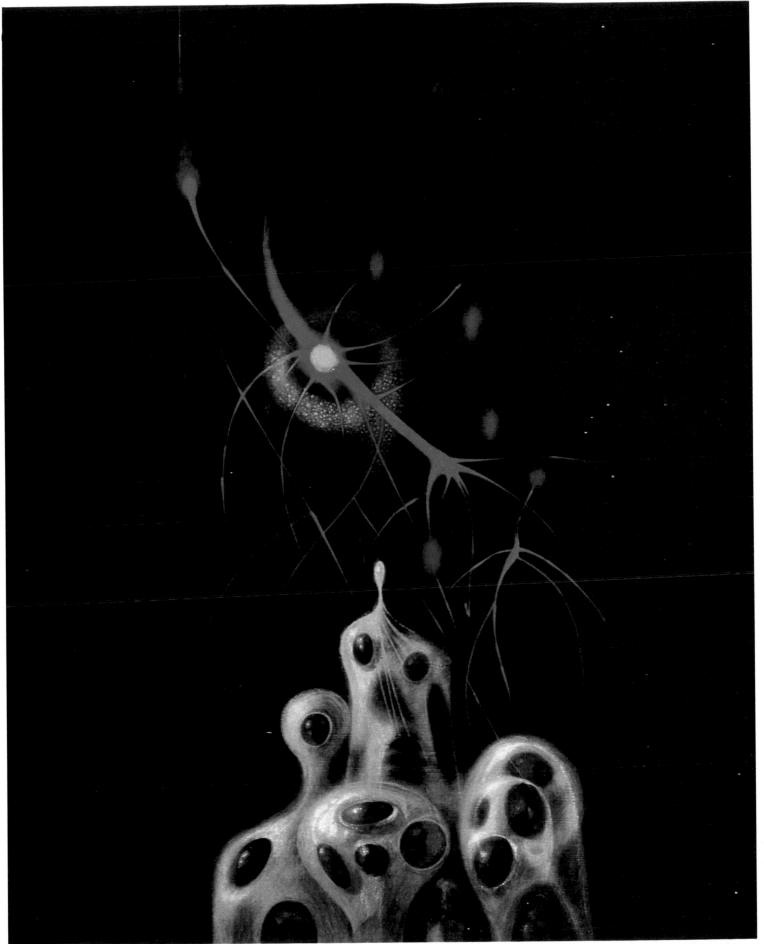

Richard Powers

Don Maitz

Paul Stinson

Darrell Sweet

Paul Alexander

Don Maitz

ASTRONAUTS

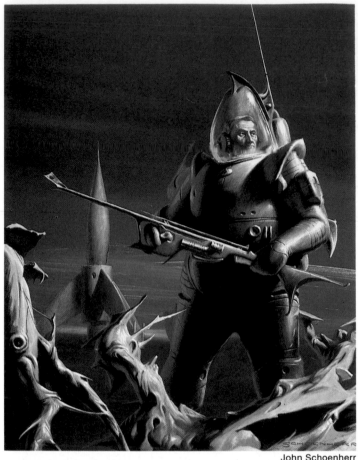

John Schoenherr

David Schleinkofer

Peter Caras

Chris Spollen

Vincent DiFate

ASTRONAUTS

John Schoenherr

John Schoenherr

Robert Petillo

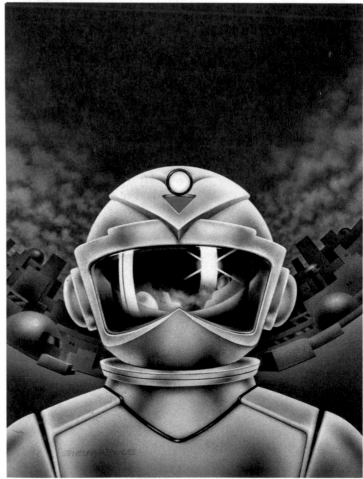

Stanislaw Fernandes

Rowena Morrill

SYMBOLISM

Charles Moll

Alan Magee

Carlos Ochagavia

Carlos Ochagavia

Charles Moll

SYMBOLISM

Edward Soyka

Jacqui Morgan

Nick Aristovulous

Nick Aristovulous

Jan Sawka

SYMBOLISM

Paul Stinson

Michael Whelan

Larry Kresek

Larry Kresek

SYMBOLISM

Chris Blumrich

Nick Aristovulous

Jerome Podwil

Carlos Ochagavia

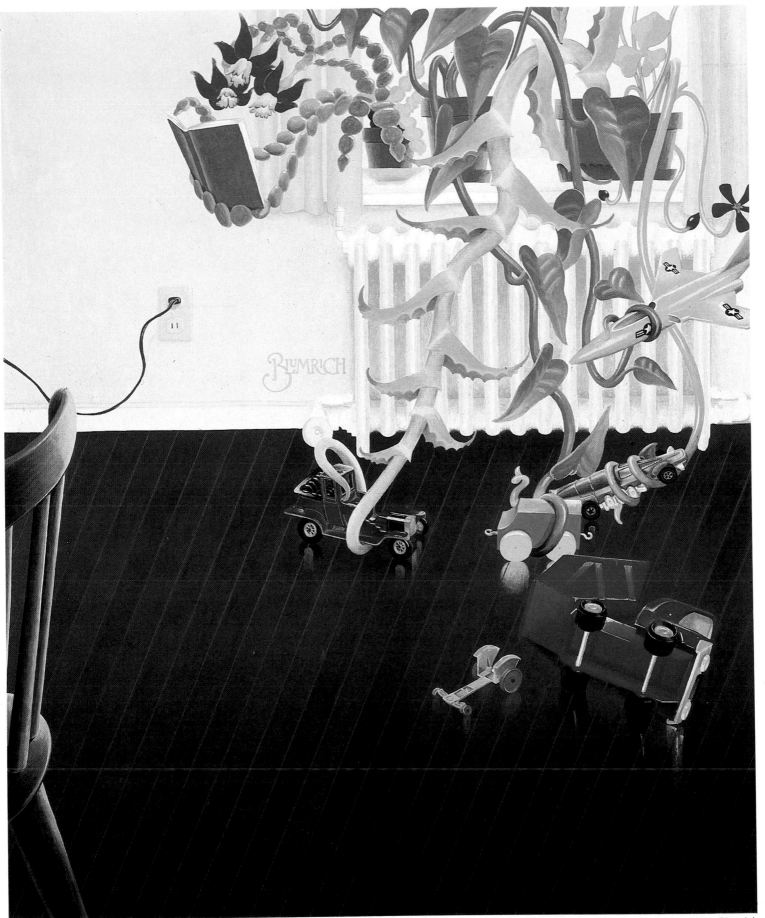

Chris Blumrich

SYMBOLISM

Nick Aristovulous

Carlos Ochagavia

Larry Kresek

Larry Kresek

John Berkey

SYMBOLISM

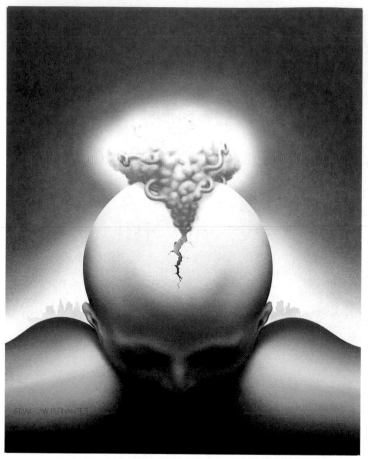

Stanislaw Fernandes

Robert Pepper

Jan Sawka

Robert Pepper

Carlos Ochagavia

SYMBOLISM

Carlos Ochagavia

Robert LoGrippo

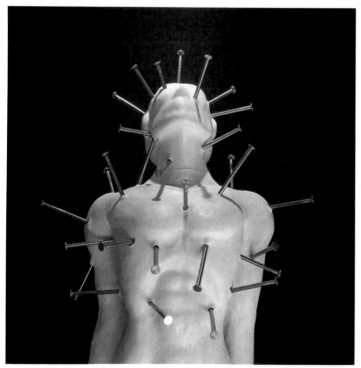

Mark Ianacone

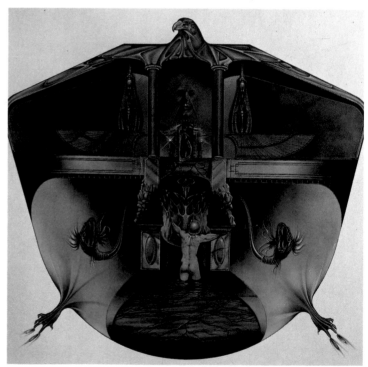

Paul Stinson

Nick Aristovulous

SYMBOLISM

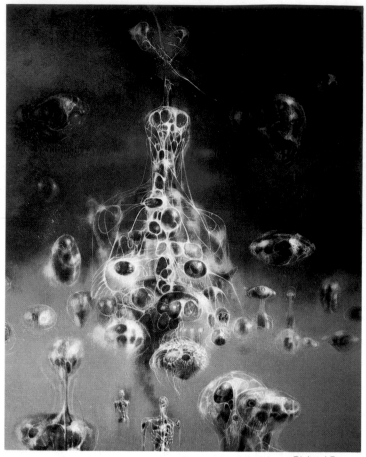

Richard Powers

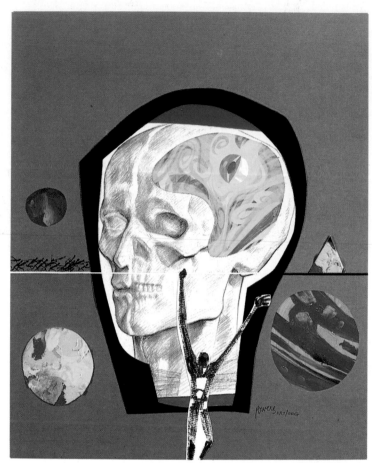

Richard Powers

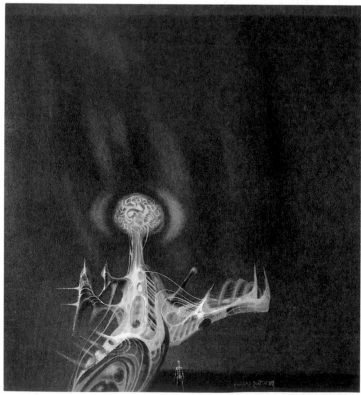

Richard Powers

Richard Powers

Richard Powers

SYMBOLISM

Nick Aristovulous

Vincent DiFate

Alan Magee

Alan Magee

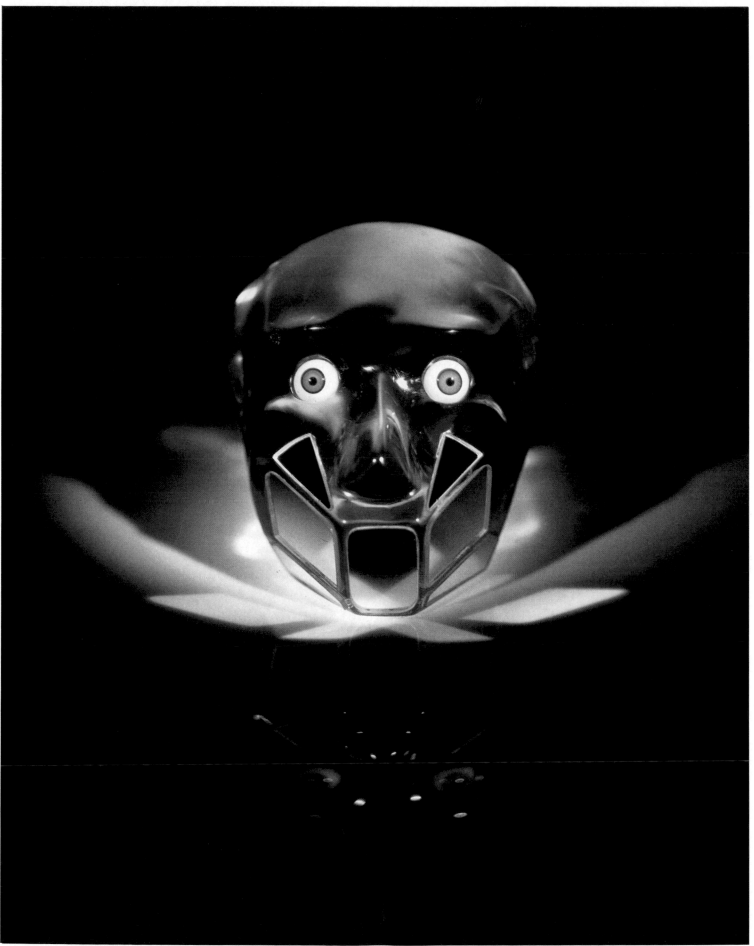

Nick Aristovulous

SYMBOLISM

Ute Osterwalder

Hans-Ulrich Osterwalder

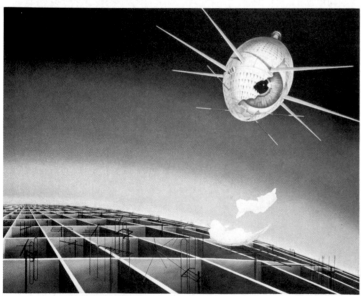

Ute Osterwalder

Ute Osterwalder

Hans-Ulrich Osterwalder

SYMBOLISM

Wilson McLean

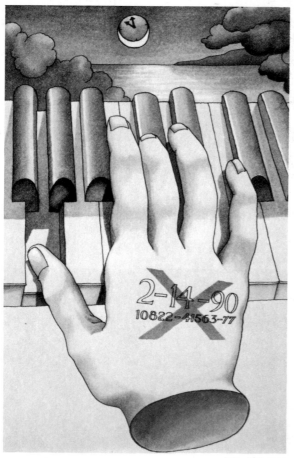

Jacqui Morgan

Jacqui Morgan

Dean Ellis

SYMBOLISM

Nick Aristovulous

Alan Magee

Jan Sawka

Jan Sawka

David Schleinkofer

SYMBOLISM

Murray Tinkelman

Brad Holland

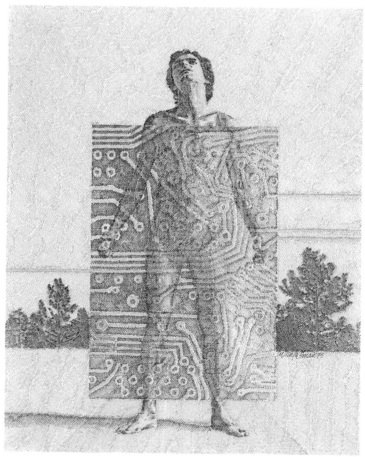

Murray Tinkelman

Brad Holland

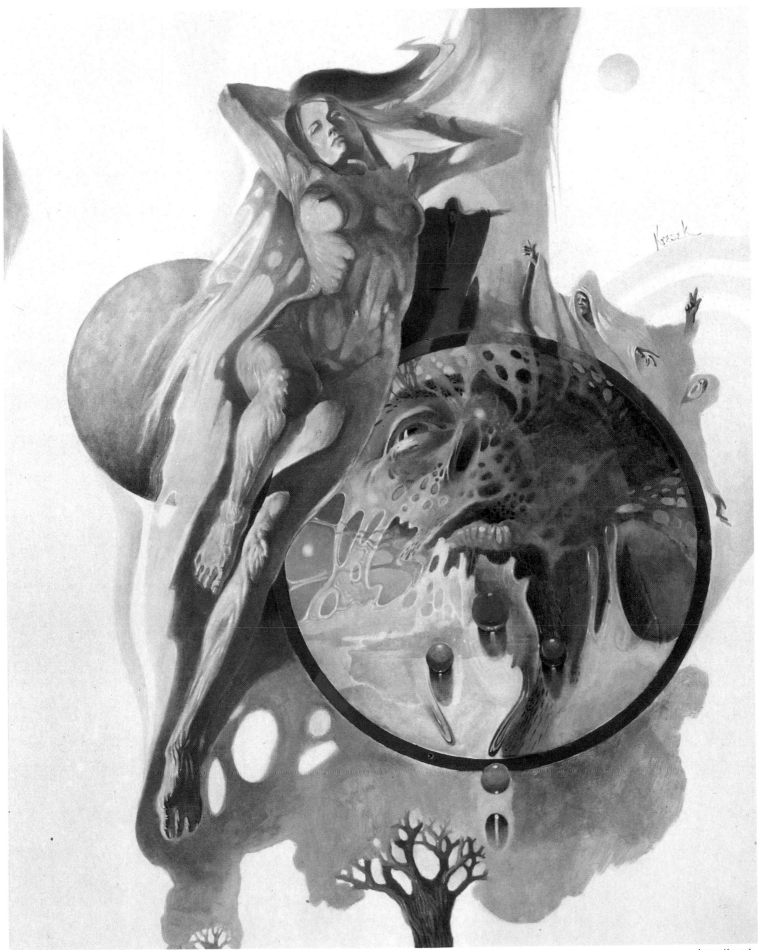

Larry Kresek

SYMBOLISM

Alan E. Cober

Alan E. Cober

Alan E. Cober

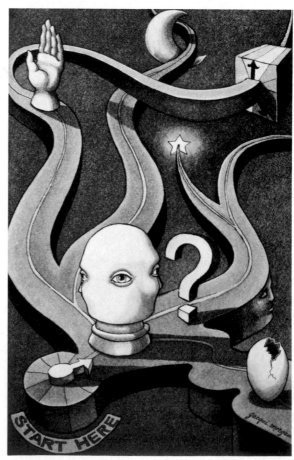

Jacqui Morgan

Rowena Morrill

SYMBOLISM

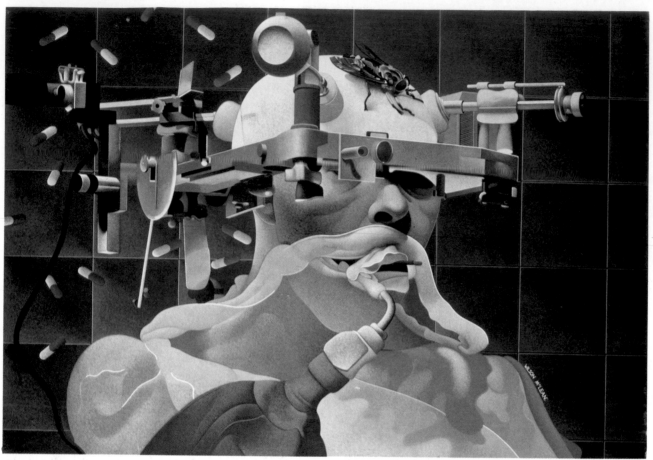

Wilson McLean

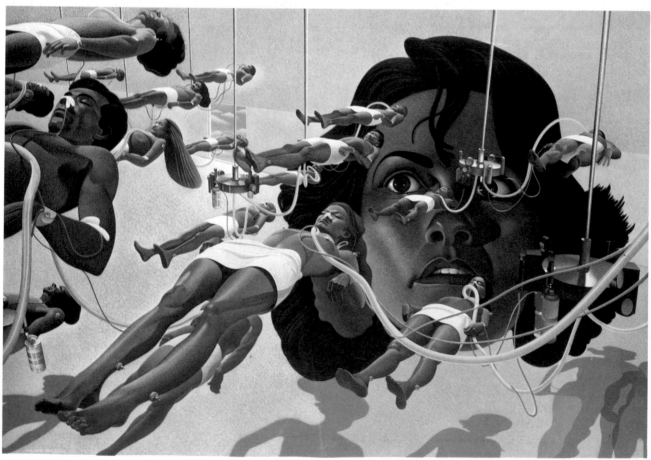

Wilson McLean

Wilson McLean

FANTASY

Douglas Beekman

Steve Hickman

Abe Echevarria

FANTASY

Murray Tinkelman

Joseph A. Smith

David McCall Johnston

Edward Soyka

FANTASY

Robert Pepper

Darrell Sweet

Darrell Sweet

Paul Stinson

FANTASY

Robert LoGrippo

Robert LoGrippo

Robert LoGrippo

FANTASY

Alan Magee

Michael Herring

Michael Herring

Michael Herring

Michael Herring

FANTASY

Wayne Barlowe

Steve Hickman

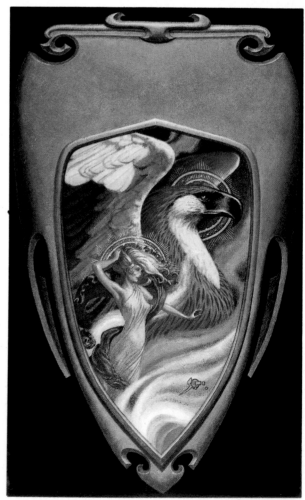

Steve Hickman

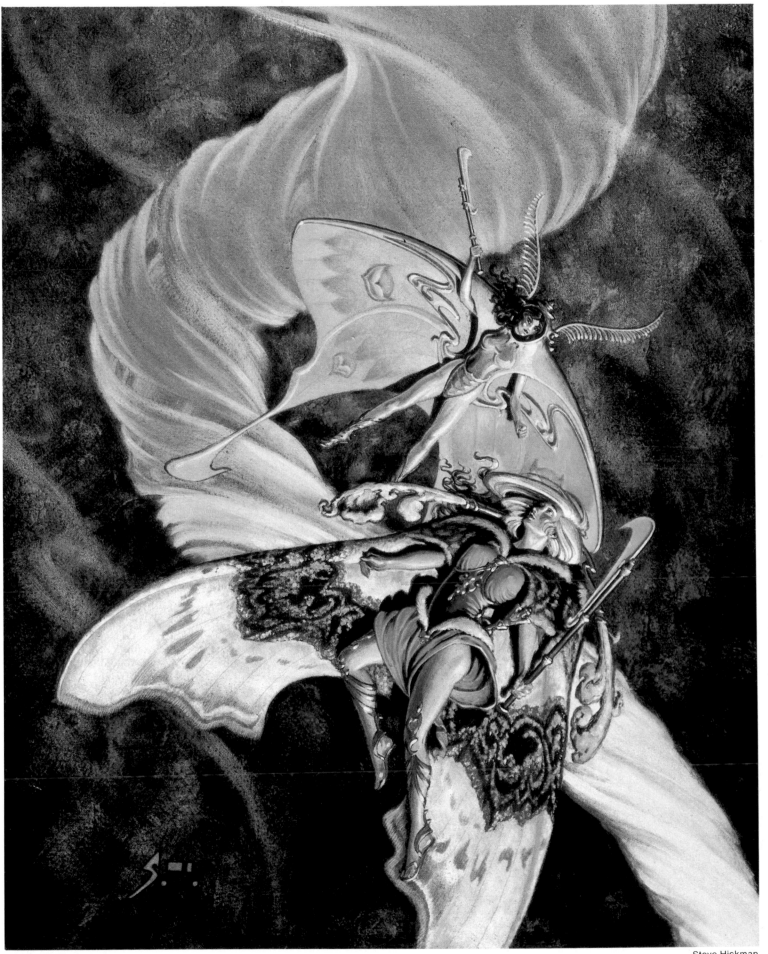

Steve Hickman

FANTASY

Edward Soyka

Carl Lundgren

Carl Lundgren

Don Ivan Punchatz

FANTASY

John Gampert

Robert LoGrippo

Jerome Podwil

BARBARIANS

Boris Vallejo

Boris Vallejo

Douglas Beekman

Douglas Beekman

Boris Vallejo

BARBARIANS

Ken Kelly

Ken Kelly

Ken Barr

Don Maitz

BARBARIANS

Paul Stinson

Wayne Barlowe

Boris Vallejo

Boris Vallejo

Boris Vallejo

BARBARIANS

Darrell Sweet

Darrell Sweet

Charles Moll

Steve Hickman

Paul Alexander

SPACECRAFT

John Berkey

John Berkey

John Berkey

SPACECRAFT

Vincent DiFate

Don Brautigam

Douglas Beekman

H. R. Van Dongen

Vincent DiFate

SPACECRAFT

John Schoenherr

Jerome Podwil

Richard Powers

Paul Lehr

SPACECRAFT

John Berkey

Paul Alexander

John Berkey

SPACECRAFT

Stanislaw Fernandes

Vernon Kramer

David McCall Johnston

Vincent DiFate

SPACECRAFT

Dean Ellis

Dean Ellis

Paul Alexander

John Berkey

SPACECRAFT

Paul Alexander

Paul Lehr

Stanislaw Fernandes

Paul Lehr

Paul Alexander

Paul Lehr

FUTUROPOLIS

Jerome Podwil

Jerome Podwil

Paul Alexander

Paul Alexander

Paul Alexander

FUTUROPOLIS

Robert Petillo

Ken Barr

Richard Powers

Carlos Ochagavia

FUTUROPOLIS

Dean Ellis

H. R. Van Dongen

Dean Ellis

John Butterfield

Ron Miller

Ron Miller

Ron Miller

OTHER WORLDS

Chris Blumrich

Hans-Ulrich Osterwalder

John Schoenherr

Richard Powers

SUPERNATURAL

Murray Tinkelman

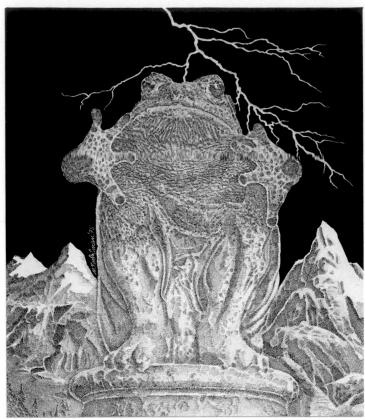

Murray Tinkelman

Abe Echevarria

Charles Moll

SUPERNATURAL

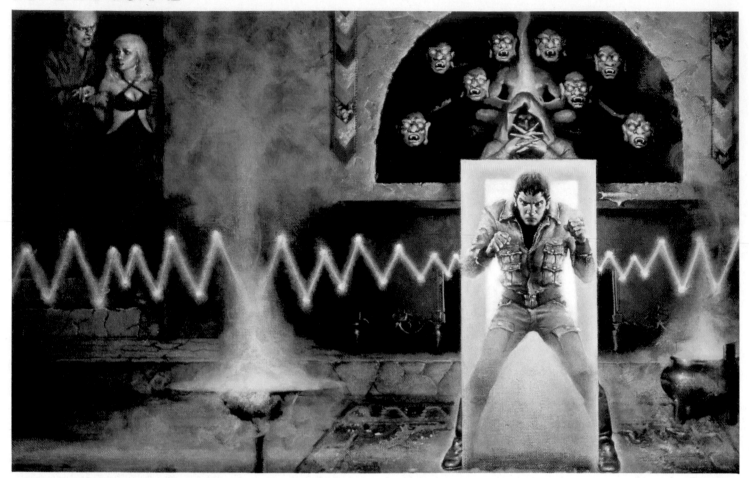

Don Maitz

Edward Soyka

Edward Soyka

Steve Hickman

SUPERNATURAL

Rowena Morrill

Rowena Morrill

Rowena Morrill

Rowena Morrill

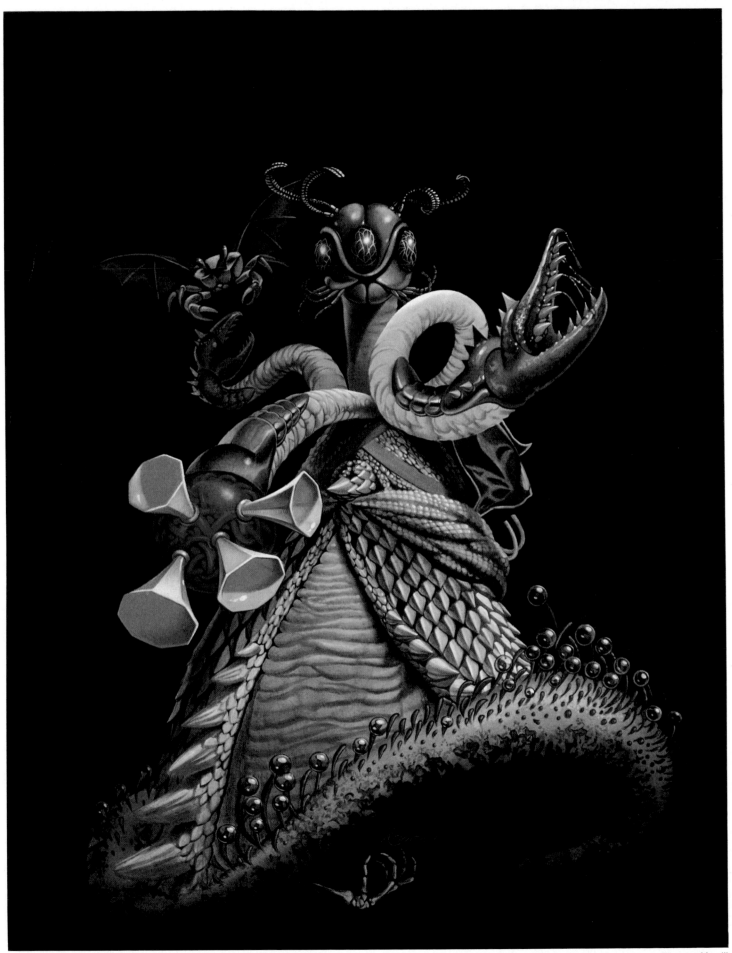

Rowena Morrill

ROBOTS

Steve Hickman

Vernon Kramer

Don Ivan Punchatz

Don Maitz

Robert Giusti

ROBOTS

Steve Hickman

Marc Phelan

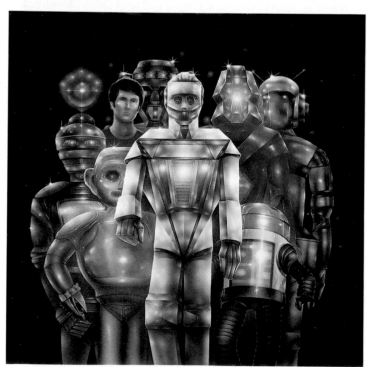

Don Brautigam

Paul Alexander

Paul Lehr

HUMOR

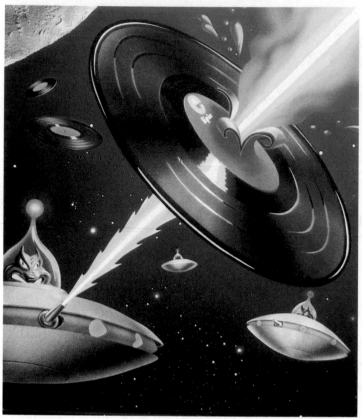

Robert Grossman

Rick Meyerowitz

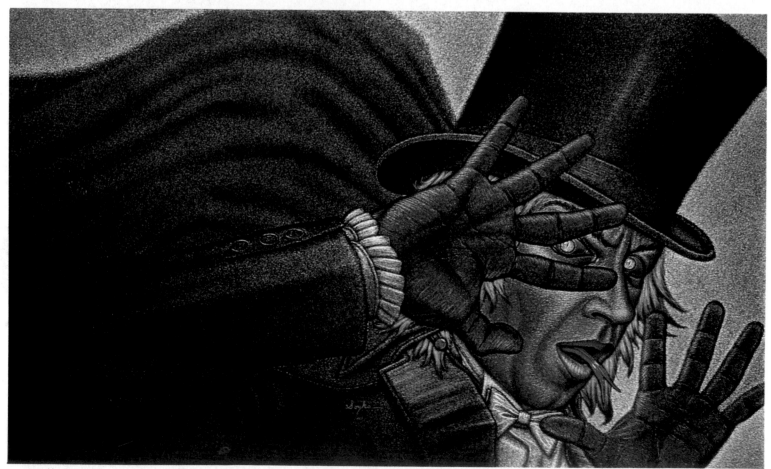

Edward Soyka

Robert Grossman

BACK TO EARTH

Jake Rajs

Jake Rajs

Jake Rajs

Jake Rajs

Vernon Kramer

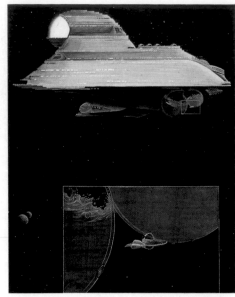

John Butterfield

Peter Caras

Mark Corcoran

Douglas Beekman

The Brothers Hildebrandt

Robert Giusti

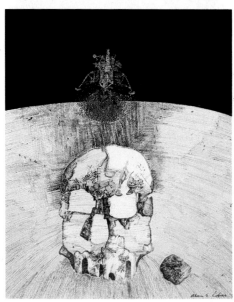

Alan E. Cober

Don Brautigam

PAGE 17

EDWARD SOYKA
Untitled
for *New England Magazine*
1977

WALTER BACHINSKY
The Perfect Lover
by Christopher Priest
Dell Publishing Company
1977

CARL LUNDGREN
The Face in the Frost
John Bellairs
Ace Books
1978

MICHAEL HERRING
Lud-in-the-Mist
by Hope Miralees
Ballantine Books / A Del Rey Book

BRAD HOLLAND
The Ace
The Illustrated Cat
Push Pin Press
1977

BRAD HOLLAND
Eldorado
The Illustrated Cat
Push Pin Press
1977

CARL LUNDGREN
The Aztec
from the artist's portfolio

JOHN GAMPERT
Untitled
based on Heinlein's *The Star Beast*
1978

VERNON KRAMER
"Recovery Area"
by David Galouye
in *Amazing Stories*
A Ziff-Davis Publication
1963

PAGE 18

JAN SAWKA
Untitled
from the artist's portfolio
1978

DAVID SCHLEINKOFER
On the Symb-Socket Circuit
by Kenneth Bulmer
Ace Books

JAN SAWKA
Untitled
from the artist's portfolio
1978

DAVID SCHLEINKOFER
Creature by the Well
from the artist's portfolio

PAGE 19

H. R. VAN DONGEN
Monsters and Medics
by James White
Ballantine Books/A Del Rey Book

PAGE 20

MARK CORCORAN
Untitled
from the artist's portfolio
1974

BRAD HOLLAND
Evening
from the artist's portfolio
1976

MARK CORCORAN
"Science Fiction Chauvinism"
by Ursula K. Le Guin
Ariel, The Book of Fantasy
1977

ABE ECHEVARRIA
The Soul of the Robot
by Barrington J. Baylew
Condor Publishing
June 1977
© 1977 Abe Echevarria

PAGE 21

DOUGLAS BEEKMAN
Untitled
from the artist's portfolio

PAGE 22

MICHAEL WHELAN
Fuzzy Sapiens
by H. Beam Piper
Ace Books
1976

MICHAEL WHELAN
"Valence Song"
in *World Without the Stars*
by Poul Anderson
Ace Books

STEVE HICKMAN
Destination Universe
by A. E. Van Vogt
Jove Publications

PAGE 23

PAUL ALEXANDER
Volteface
by Mark Adlard
Ace Books

PAGE 24

JOSÉ CRUZ
Untitled
from the artist's portfolio
1976

RAY FEIBUSH
Untitled
New English Library
1975

RAY FEIBUSH
Untitled
for H. G. Toys
1978

RAY FEIBUSH
"Death Beast"
by David Gerrold
in *Star Log Magazine*
1978

PAGE 25

RAY FEIBUSH
Untitled
for H. G. Toys
1978

APPENDIX

PAGE 26

H. R. VAN DONGEN
The Siege of Wonder
by Mark Geston
DAW Books
1977

JOSEPH A. SMITH
Untitled
from the artist's portfolio

VINCENT DI FATE
The Tritonian Ring
by L. Sprague de Camp
Ballantine Books/A Del Rey Book

H. R. VAN DONGEN
A Specter is Haunting Texas
by Fritz Leiber
DAW Books
1977

PAGE 27

DON MAITZ
None But Man
by Gordon R. Dickson
DAW Books
1977

PAGE 28

WILSON McLEAN
Untitled
from the artist's portfolio

PAUL ALEXANDER
The Monadic Universe
by George Zebrowski
Ace Books

PAUL ALEXANDER
Untitled
from the artist's portfolio

PAGE 29

MICHAEL PRESLEY
Light at the End of the Universe
by Terry Carr
Pyramid Books

PAGE 30

WAYNE BARLOWE
Untitled
from the artist's portfolio

HARRY BENNETT
The Lomokome Papers
by Herman Wouk
Pocket Books
1975

ROBERT PETILLO
from the artist's portfolio
based on *Heavy Planet*
by Milton Rothman
1978

MICHAEL PRESLEY
Untitled
from the artist's portfolio
1977

PAGE 31

DON IVAN PUNCHATZ
Untitled
from the artist's portfolio

PAGE 32

H. R. VAN DONGEN
Survival Game
by Colin Kapp
Ballantine Books/A Del Rey Book

H. R. VAN DONGEN
A Jungle of Stars
by Jack L. Chalker
Ballantine Books/A Del Rey Book

H. R. VAN DONGEN
Mission to Universe
by Gordon R. Dickson
Ballantine Books/A Del Rey Book

H. R. VAN DONGEN
The Jupiter Theft
by Donald Moffitt
Ballantine Books/A Del Rey Book

PAGE 33

PAUL ALEXANDER
Get Off the Unicorn
by Anne McCaffrey
Ballantine Books/A Del Rey Book

PAGE 34

DARRELL SWEET
Decision at Doona
by Anne McCaffrey
Ballantine Books/A Del Rey Book

THE BROTHERS HILDEBRANDT
Untitled
from the artist's portfolio

ROBERT PETILLO
from the artist's portfolio
based on *A Martian Odyssey*
by Stanley Weinbaum
1977

DARRELL SWEET
A Case of Conscience
by James Blish
Ballantine Books/A Del Rey Book

PAGE 35

THE BROTHERS HILDEBRANDT
Restoree
by Anne McCaffrey
Ballantine Books/A Del Rey Book

PAGE 36

BRAD HOLLAND
The Elder
from the artist's portfolio
1978

WAYNE BARLOWE
The Cold Cash War
by Robert Asprin
Dell Publishing Company
1978

PETER CARAS
Smart as the Devil
by Felice Picano
Dell Publishing Company
1978

H. R. VAN DONGEN
Mission of Gravity
by Hal Clement
Ballantine Books/A Del Rey Book

PAGE 37

JOHN SCHOENHERR
"Baron Harkonnen"
from *Dune*
by Frank Herbert
Berkley Publishing Corporation

JOHN SCHOENHERR
"Stilgaar and the Freemen"
from *Dune*
by Frank Herbert
Berkley Publishing Corporation

PAGE 38 _____

DARRELL SWEET
The Long Tomorrow
by Leigh Brackett
Ballantine Books/A Del Rey Book

CHRIS SPOLLEN
Untitled
for *Bananas Magazine*

H. R. VAN DONGEN
The Best of Fredric Brown
edited by Robert Bloch
Ballantine Books/A Del Rey Book

PAGE 39 _____

PAUL LEHR
Dorsai!
by Gordon R. Dickson
DAW Books

PAGE 40 _____

MICHAEL WHELAN
Time and Again
by Clifford D. Simak
Ace Books

KEN BARR
for *Hot Stuff #4 Magazine*
Published by Sol Quartuccio

STEVE HICKMAN
Doctor to the Stars
by Murray Leinster
Jove Publications

KEN BARR
Road to the Rim
by A. Bertram Chandler
Ace Books

PAGE 41 _____

ROBERT SCHULTZ
Untitled
from the artist's portfolio

PAGE 42 _____

JAN SAWKA
Untitled
from the artist's portfolio
1978

DON BRAUTIGAM
Michaelmas
by A.J. Budrys
Berkley Publishing Corporation
1978

STANISLAW FERNANDES
Sturgeon in Orbit
by Theodore Sturgeon
Pyramid Books
1977

DON BRAUTIGAM
Time Gate
by John Jakes
Signet Books
1977

PAGE 43 _____

RICHARD POWERS
Star Light, Star Bright
by Alfred Bester
Berkley Publishing Corporation

PAGE 44 _____

DON MAITZ
Gods of Xuma
by David J. Lake
DAW Books
1977

DARRELL SWEET
Inherit the Stars
by James P. Hogan
Ballantine Books/A Del Rey Book

PAUL STINSON
Untitled
from the artist's portfolio

PAUL ALEXANDER
Untitled
for David Publishing

PAGE 45 _____

DON MAITZ
Catchworld
by Chris Boyce
Fawcett
1978

PAGE 46 _____

JOHN SCHOENHERR
Untitled
from the artist's portfolio

PETER CARAS
Untitled
from *The Avenger*
by Kenneth Robeson
Warner Books

DAVID SCHLEINKOFER
*Casey Agonistes and other
Science Fiction Stories*
by Richard McKenna
Ace Books

CHRIS SPOLLEN
"The Feminine Imperative"
by Marion Zimmer Bradley
for *Viva Magazine*
December 1977

PAGE 47 _____

VINCENT DI FATE
Showboat World
by Jack Vance
Pyramid Books
1974

PAGE 48 _____

JOHN SCHOENHERR
Untitled
for *Analog Magazine*

ROBERT PETILLO
Untitled
from the artist's portfolio
1978

JOHN SCHOENHERR
"The Trouble with Telstar"
for *Analog Magazine*

STANISLAW FERNANDES
Rendezvous with Rama
by Arthur C. Clarke
Ballantine Books/A Del Rey Book

PAGE 49 _____

ROWENA MORRILL
The Dreaming Jewels
by Theodore Sturgeon
Dell Publishing Company

APPENDIX

PAGE 50 _____

CHARLES MOLL
Wandering Stars
edited by Jack Dann
Pocket Books
1975

CARLOS OCHAGAVIA
Alpha Centauri or Die
by Leigh Brackett
Ace Books

ALAN MAGEE
The Undead
edited by James Dickey
Pocket Books

CARLOS OCHAGAVIA
Venus Development
by David Bergamini
Popular Library

PAGE 51 _____

CHARLES MOLL
No Direction Home
by Norman Spinrad
Pocket Books
1974

PAGE 52 _____

EDWARD SOYKA
for *Emergency Medicine Magazine*

NICK ARISTOVULOUS
Broken Hearts
for MBA Communications
1977

JACQUI MORGAN
The Birth of the Ear
for Sansui Electronics
1976

NICK ARISTOVULOUS
"MBA Motivation Survey"
MBA Communications
1978

PAGE 53 _____

JAN SAWKA
Untitled
from the artist's portfolio
1977

PAGE 54 _____

PAUL STINSON
Middle Earth
from the artist's portfolio

LARRY KRESEK
Untitled
from the artist's portfolio

MICHAEL WHELAN
City
by Clifford D. Simak
Ace Books

PAGE 55 _____

LARRY KRESEK
Untitled
from the artist's portfolio

PAGE 56 _____

CHRIS BLUMRICH
Adventure Weekends
from the artist's portfolio
© 1975 Christoph Blumrich

JEROME PODWIL
Here and Hereafter
by Ruth Montgomery
Fawcett

NICK ARISTOVULOUS
Beethoven's Ninth Symphony
for RCA Records
1972

CARLOS OCHAGAVIA
Untitled
from the artist's portfolio

PAGE 57 _____

CHRIS BLUMRICH
Barney was Alarmed by His Garden
from the artist's portfolio
© Christoph Blumrich 1974

PAGE 58 _____

NICK ARISTOVULOUS
"In The Year 2025"
by Zager and Evan
RCA Records
1976

LARRY KRESEK
Untitled
from the artist's portfolio

CARLOS OCHAGAVIA
A Scanner Darkly
by Philip K. Dick
Ballantine Books/A Del Rey Book

LARRY KRESEK
Untitled
for Servitus Medical Supplies

PAGE 59 _____

JOHN BERKEY
Star Fire
by Ingo Swann
Dell Publishing Company
1969

PAGE 60 _____

STANISLAW FERNANDES
Cirque
by Terry Carr
Fawcett

JAN SAWKA
Untitled
from the artist's portfolio
1978

ROBERT PEPPER
Ellison in Wonderland
by Harlan Ellison
New American Library

ROBERT PEPPER
Starburst
by Alfred Bester
New American Library

PAGE 61 _____

CARLOS OCHAGAVIA
for *New Times Magazine*

APPENDIX

PAGE 62 _____

CARLOS OCHAGAVIA
Untitled
from the artist's portfolio

MARK IANACONE
"Torture"
in *Gallery Magazine*
May 1978

ROBERT LO GRIPPO
Untitled
from the artist's portfolio

PAUL STINSON
Untitled
from the artist's portfolio

PAGE 63 _____

NICK ARISTOVULOUS
Sssssss
Unpublished movie poster
for Communications Quorum
1974

PAGE 64 _____

RICHARD POWERS
Cloudcry
by Joyce Van Scyoc
Berkley Publishing Corporation

RICHARD POWERS
Maske: Thaery
by Jack Vance
Berkley Publishing Corporation

RICHARD POWERS
Untitled
Berkley Publishing Corporation

RICHARD POWERS
Star Light, Star Bright Vol. I
by Alfred Bester
Berkley Publishing Corporation

PAGE 65 _____

RICHARD POWERS
Untitled
from the artist's portfolio

PAGE 66 _____

NICK ARISTOVULOUS
Untitled
from the artist's portfolio
1978

ALAN MAGEE
Roadside Picnic, Tales of the Troika
by Arkady and Boris Strugatsky
Pocket Books

VINCENT DI FATE
Broke Down Engine
by Ron Goulart
Macmillan Publishing Company
1970

ALAN MAGEE
Time of the Assassins
by Henry Miller
Pocket Books

PAGE 67 _____

NICK ARISTOVULOUS
In the Wake of Man
by R.A. Lafferty, Gene Wolfe,
   and Walter Moody
Bobbs-Merrill Publishers
1975

PAGE 68 _____

UTE OSTERWALDER
for *HOERZU Magazine*
© 1973 Ute Osterwalder

UTE OSTERWALDER
"A New Star on Heaven"
by W.H. Hodgson
in *Playboy Magazine*
1973
Heinrich Bauer Verlag

HANS-ULRICH OSTERWALDER
Malpertuis
by Jean Ray
Sahrkamp Verlag-Insel
© 1973 Hans-Ulrich Osterwalder

UTE OSTERWALDER
The Voice of Night
by W.H. Hodgson
Sahrkamp Verlag-Insel
© 1969 Ute Osterwalder

PAGE 69 _____

HANS-ULRICH OSTERWALDER
Traitor to the Living
© 1970 Hans-Ulrich Osterwalder

PAGE 70 _____

WILSON McLEAN
Untitled
from the artist's portfolio

JACQUI MORGAN
"Terrafied"
by Arthur Tofte
from *Children of Infinity*
edited by Roger Elwood
Franklin Watts
1973

JACQUI MORGAN
"Half Life"
by Rachel Payes
from *Children of Infinity*
edited by Roger Elwood
Franklin Watts
1973

PAGE 71 _____

DEAN ELLIS
Agent of Chaos
from the artist's portfolio

PAGE 72 _____

NICK ARISTOVULOUS
"Ultradian Rhythm"
in *Psychology Today Magazine*
1977

JAN SAWKA
Untitled
from the artist's portfolio
1978

ALAN MAGEE
Clea
by Lawrence Durrell
Pocket Books

JAN SAWKA
Untitled
from the artist's portfolio
1978

PAGE 73 _____

DAVID SCHLEINKOFER
The Preserving Machine
by Philip K. Dick
Ace Books
1976

APPENDIX

PAGE 74 _____

MURRAY TINKELMAN
The Sheep Look Up
by John Brunner
Ballantine Books/A Del Rey Book

MURRAY TINKELMAN
The Shockwave Rider
by John Brunner
Ballantine Books/A Del Rey Book

BRAD HOLLAND
The Lone Wolf
from *Human Scandals*
by Brad Holland
T. Y. Crowell Publishers
1977

BRAD HOLLAND
My Larval Years
from the artist's portfolio
1971

PAGE 75 _____

LARRY KRESEK
Untitled
from the artist's portfolio
1972

PAGE 76 _____

ALAN E. COBER
Untitled
from the artist's portfolio
1974

ALAN E. COBER
for *The American Way Magazine*
American Airlines

ALAN E. COBER
for *Creative Living Magazine*
1977

JACQUI MORGAN
"A Game of Futures"
by Lester del Rey
from *Children of Infinity*
edited by Roger Elwood
Franklin Watts
1973

PAGE 77 _____

ROWENA MORRILL
Nightwalk
by Bob Shaw
Dell Publishing Company

PAGE 78 _____

WILSON McLEAN
"Science Without Shame"
in *Oui Magazine*
March 1976

WILSON McLEAN
Coma
Unpublished movie poster
1977

PAGE 79 _____

WILSON McLEAN
for *Saturday Review*

PAGE 80 _____

DOUGLAS BEEKMAN
Untitled
from the artist's portfolio

STEVE HICKMAN
The Warlock In Spite of Himself
by Christopher Stashef
Ace Books

PAGE 81 _____

ABE ECHEVARRIA
Untitled
for A.E. Productions
© 1978 Abe Echevarria

PAGE 82 _____

MURRAY TINKELMAN
The Whole Man
by John Brunner
Ballantine Books/A Del Rey Book

DAVID McCALL JOHNSTON
New Worlds for Old
edited by Lin Carter
Ballantine Books

JOSEPH A. SMITH
Untitled
from the artist's portfolio
© 1977 Joseph A. Smith

PAGE 83 _____

EDWARD SOYKA
for ESP Disc
© 1971 Edward Soyka

PAGE 84 _____

ROBERT PEPPER
Hrolf-Kraki's Saga
by Poul Anderson
Ballantine Books

DARRELL SWEET
Hrolf-Kraki's Saga
by Poul Anderson
Ballantine Books/A Del Rey Book

DARRELL SWEET
Blue Star
by Fletcher Pratt
Ballantine Books/A Del Rey Book

PAGE 85 _____

PAUL STINSON
He
from the artist's portfolio

PAGE 86 _____

ROBERT LO GRIPPO
Untitled
from the artist's portfolio
1970

ROBERT LO GRIPPO
Taming Blue Water Terrain
Motorboat & Sailing Magazine
1978

PAGE 87 _____

ROBERT LO GRIPPO
Untitled
from the artist's portfolio
1972

APPENDIX

PAGE 88

ALAN MAGEE
*The Secret Life of Algernon
   Pendleton*
by Russell Greenan
Fawcett World Library
1977

MICHAEL HERRING
Wisdom's Daughter
by H. Rider Haggard
Ballantine Books/A Del Rey Book

MICHAEL HERRING
The Blue Hawk
by Peter Dickinson
Ballantine Books/A Del Rey Book

MICHAEL HERRING
World's Desire
by H. Rider Haggard
Ballantine Books/A Del Rey Book

PAGE 89

MICHAEL HERRING
The Mask of Circe
by Henry Kuttner
Ace Books

PAGE 90

WAYNE BARLOWE
Untitled
from the artist's portfolio

STEVE HICKMAN
Untitled
from the artist's portfolio

STEVE HICKMAN
The Weirwoods
by Thomas Burnett Swann
Ace Books

PAGE 91

STEVE HICKMAN
Moondust
by Thomas Burnett Swann
Ace Books

PAGE 92

EDWARD SOYKA
Or, All the Seas with Oysters
by Avram Davidson
Pocket Books

CARL LUNDGREN
The Monument
from the artist's portfolio

CARL LUNDGREN
The Light of Barbrin
by Joseph Burgo
Pocket Books

PAGE 93

DON IVAN PUNCHATZ
Untitled
from the artist's portfolio

PAGE 94

JOHN GAMPERT
The Whore of Babylon, Long Island
from the artist's portfolio
1978

ROBERT LO GRIPPO
Untitled
from the artist's portfolio
1971

PAGE 95

JEROME PODWIL
This Perfect Day
from the artist's portfolio

PAGE 96

BORIS VALLEJO
Behind the Walls of Terror
1971

DOUGLAS BEEKMAN
Untitled
Berkley Publishing Corporation

BORIS VALLEJO
The Best of Leigh Brackett
Ballantine Books/A Del Rey Book

DOUGLAS BEEKMAN
Planet Patrol
by Sonya Dorman
Berkley Publishing Corporation

PAGE 97

BORIS VALLEJO
The Flight of the Horse
by Larry Niven
Ballantine Books/A Del Rey Book

PAGE 98

KEN KELLY
Hour of the Dragon
by Robert E. Howard
Berkley Publishing Corporation
1978

KEN BARR
The Guns of Avalone
by Roger Zelazny
Avon Books

KEN KELLY
Red Nails
by Robert E. Howard
Berkley Publishing Corporation
1978

PAGE 99

DON MAITZ
*"Barbarians to Black Magicians"
Flashing Swords #4*
edited by Lin Carter
Dell Publishing Company

PAGE 100

PAUL STINSON
The Eternal Champion
from the artist's portfolio

BORIS VALLEJO
Demon in the Mirror
from the artist's portfolio
1977

WAYNE BARLOWE
Untitled
from the artist's portfolio

BORIS VALLEJO
Nubian Warrior
from the artist's portfolio
1978

PAGE 101

BORIS VALLEJO
In the Underworld
from the artist's portfolio
1978

APPENDIX

PAGE 102

DARRELL SWEET
The Doomfarers of Coramonde
by Brian Daley
Ballantine Books/A Del Rey Book

CHARLES MOLL
The Best of Jack Vance
by Jack Vance
Pocket Books
1977

DARRELL SWEET
Citizen of the Galaxy
by Robert Heinlein
Ballantine Books/A Del Rey Book

STEVE HICKMAN
Norhala of the Lightnings
from the artist's portfolio
© 1977 Steve Hickman

PAGE 103

PAUL ALEXANDER
Untitled
from the artist's portfolio

PAGE 104

JOHN BERKEY
Under Pressure
by Frank Herbert
Ballantine Books

JOHN BERKEY
Colonies in Space
by T. A. Heppenheimer
Warner Books
1978

PAGE 105

JOHN BERKEY
Spartan Planet
by A. Bertram Chandler
Dell Publishing Company
1969

PAGE 106

VINCENT DI FATE
The Chaos Weapon
by Colin Kapp
Ballantine Books/A Del Rey Book

DOUGLAS BEEKMAN
Untitled
from the artist's portfolio

DON BRAUTIGAM
Sargasso of Space
by Andre Norton
Ace Books
1977

H. R. VAN DONGEN
Starlight
by Hal Clement
Ballantine Books/A Del Rey Book

PAGE 107

VINCENT DI FATE
The Best of Philip K. Dick
Ballantine Books/A Del Rey Book
1977

PAGE 108

JEROME PODWIL
The Other Side of Time
by Keith Laumer
Signet Books

RICHARD POWERS
Untitled
from the artist's portfolio

JOHN SCHOENHERR
for *Analog Magazine*

PAGE 109

PAUL LEHR
Starship Troopers
by Robert Heinlein
Berkley Publishing Corporation

PAGE 110

JOHN BERKEY
Star SF #2
edited by Frederik Pohl
Ballantine Books
1972

PAUL ALEXANDER
for *Institutions Magazine*
Cahners Publishing Company

PAGE 111

JOHN BERKEY
Star SF #5
edited by Frederik Pohl
Ballantine Books
1972

PAGE 112

STANISLAW FERNANDES
Star Diaries
by Stanislaw Lem
Abrams Books
1977

DAVID McCALL JOHNSTON
20,000 Leagues Under the Sea
by Jules Verne
for the Franklin Mint
1977

VERNON KRAMER
Neither Stairs nor Door
by Robert F. Young
Fantastic Magazine
January 1963

PAGE 113

VINCENT DI FATE
Future Fears
for *Analog Magazine*

PAGE 114

DEAN ELLIS
Untitled
from the artist's portfolio

PAUL ALEXANDER
Untitled
for *Encyclopedia Britannica*
1977 Yearbook

DEAN ELLIS
Tales from the White Hart
by Arthur C. Clarke
Ballantine Books

PAGE 115

JOHN BERKEY
Untitled
from the artist's portfolio

APPENDIX

PAGE 116_____

PAUL ALEXANDER
for New Jersey Telephone Co.

PAUL LEHR
Untitled
from the artist's portfolio

PAGE 117 _____

STANISLAW FERNANDES
Prelude to Space
by Arthur C. Clarke
Ballantine Books/A Del Rey Book

PAGE 118_____

PAUL LEHR
for *Quest Magazine*
January 1978

PAUL ALEXANDER
Untitled
from the artist's portfolio

PAGE 119_____

PAUL LEHR
Untitled
from the artist's portfolio

PAGE 120_____

JEROME PODWIL
The Enemy Stars
by Poul Anderson
Berkley Publishing Corporation

PAUL ALEXANDER
The Worlds of Frank Herbert
by Frank Herbert
Berkley Publishing Corporation

JEROME PODWIL
The Players of Null A
by A. E. Van Vogt
Berkley Publishing Corporation

PAUL ALEXANDER
Untitled
Popular Library

PAGE 121_____

PAUL ALEXANDER
Untitled
from the artist's portfolio

PAGE 122_____

ROBERT PETILLO
The Merry Andrew
from the artist's portfolio

KEN BARR
Wolfbane
by Frederik Pohl & C.M. Kornbluth
Bantam Books

RICHARD POWERS
Pstalemate
by Lester del Rey
Berkley Publishing Corporation

PAGE 123_____

CARLOS OCHAGAVIA
for *New Times Magazine*

PAGE 124_____

DEAN ELLIS
Untitled
from the artist's portfolio

H. R. VAN DONGEN
Undersea Quest
by Frederik Pohl and Jack
   Williamson
Ballantine Books/A Del Rey Book

PAGE 125_____

DEAN ELLIS
Analog Magazine

PAGE 126_____

JOHN BUTTERFIELD
from *The Extraterrestrial Report*
by John Butterfield and
   Richard Siegel
A & W Visual Press
© 1978 Butterfield, Siegel
   and Suarez

RON MILLER
*The Milky Way Galaxy (as Seen
from a Planet on the Small
Magellic Cloud)*
© 1977 Ron Miller

PAGE 127_____

RON MILLER
In the Martian Highlands
© 1977 Ron Miller

RON MILLER
Saturn as Seen from Rhea
© 1977 Ron Miller

PAGE 128_____

CHRIS BLUMRICH
White Elephants
for *Forbes Magazine*
© 1977 Christoph Blumrich

JOHN SCHOENHERR
"Sietch Tabr"
from *Dune*
by Frank Herbert
Berkley Publishing Corporation

HANS-ULRICH OSTERWALDER
The House at the Borderland
by William Hope Hodgson
Sahrkamp Verlag-Insel
© 1972 Osterwalder

PAGE 129_____

RICHARD POWERS
The Shape Changers
by Keith Laumer
Berkley Publishing Corporation

PAGE 130_____

MURRAY TINKELMAN
Lovecraft, A Biography
by L. Sprague de Camp
Ballantine Books/A Del Rey Book

ABE ECHEVARRIA
Devil Pack
from *Tales of the Unexpected*
NBC-TV
June 1977

MURRAY TINKELMAN
*The Horror in the Museum and
   Other Revisions*
by H.P. Lovecraft and others
Ballantine Books/A Del Rey Book

PAGE 131_____

CHARLES MOLL
Visions of Tomorrow
edited by Roger Elwood
Pocket Books
1976

APPENDIX

PAGE 132

DON MAITZ
Untitled
from the artist's portfolio

EDWARD SOYKA
By The North Door
by Meg Elizabeth Atkins
Ballantine Books

EDWARD SOYKA
The Best of Harry Harrison
by Harry Harrison
Pocket Books

PAGE 133

STEVE HICKMAN
The King in Yellow
by Robert W. Chambers
Ace Books

PAGE 134

ROWENA MORRILL
Isabel
by Jane Parkhurst
Jove Publications

ROWENA MORRILL
Isabel
by Jane Parkhurst
Jove Publications

ROWENA MORRILL
The Dunwich Horror
by H.P. Lovecraft
Jove Publications

ROWENA MORRILL
*The Dark Dimensions and the
    Rim Gods*
by A. Bertram Chandler
Ace Books

PAGE 135

ROWENA MORRILL
The Colour Out of Space
by H.P. Lovecraft
Jove Publications

PAGE 136

STEVE HICKMAN
The Gasm #3
from the artist's portfolio
1978

DON IVAN PUNCHATZ
Untitled
from the artist's portfolio

VERNON KRAMER
Untitled
from the artist's portfolio

DON MAITZ
*Lucky Starr and the Big Sun
    of Mercury*
by Paul French
Fawcett

PAGE 137

ROBERT GIUSTI
Who?
by Algis Budrys
Ballantine Books / A Del Rey Book

PAGE 138

STEVE HICKMAN
Untitled
from the artist's portfolio

DON BRAUTIGAM
*Eight Stories from the Rest of
    the Robots*
by Isaac Asimov
Jove Publications

MARC PHELAN
Untitled
from the artist's portfolio

PAUL ALEXANDER
Visible Man
by Gardner Dozois
Berkley Publishing Corporation

PAGE 139

PAUL LEHR
A Choice of Gods
by Clifford D. Simak
Berkley Publishing Corporation

PAGE 140

ROBERT GROSSMAN
Untitled
from the artist's portfolio

EDWARD SOYKA
The Phantom of the Opera
for Private Stock Records

RICK MEYEROWITZ
Nellie Collins
from the artist's portfolio

PAGE 141

ROBERT GROSSMAN
Dark Star
by Alan Dean Foster
Ballantine Books / A Del Rey Book

PAGE 142

JAKE RAJS
Badlands
from the photographer's portfolio
© DAO 1978

JAKE RAJS
Future City
from the photographer's portfolio
© DAO 1978

JAKE RAJS
Driving into the Night
from the photographer's portfolio
© DAO 1978

PAGE 143

JAKE RAJS
Sand and Butte
from the photographer's portfolio
© DAO 1978

PAGE 144

VERNON KRAMER
Garden of Fear
by R. E. Howard
Fantastic Magazine
A Ziff-Davis Publication
May 1961

MARK CORCORAN
Alien Roundup
from *The Extraterrestrial Report*
by Butterfield and Siegel
A & W Visual Press
© 1978 Butterfield, Siegel and Suarez

ROBERT GIUSTI
It's Alive
by Richard Woodley
Ballantine Books

JOHN BUTTERFIELD
From *The Extraterrestrial Report*
by Butterfield and Siegel
A & W Visual Press
© 1978 Butterfield, Siegel and Suarez

DOUGLAS BEEKMAN
Untitled
for *Heavy Metal Magazine*
October 1978

ALAN E. COBER
Untitled
from the artist's portfolio

PETER CARAS
Untitled
from *The Avenger*
by Kenneth Robeson
Warner Books

THE BROTHERS HILDEBRANDT
The Early del Rey, Vol. I
by Lester del Rey
Ballantine Books/A Del Rey Book

DON BRAUTIGAM
Abominable Snowmen
by Ivan T. Sanderson
Jove Publications
1977

Paul Alexander 23, 28, 33, 44, 103, 110, 114, 116, 118, 120, 121, 138
Nick Aristovulous 52, 56, 58, 63, 66, 67, 72
Walter Bachinsky 17
Wayne Barlowe 30, 36, 90, 100
Ken Barr 40, 98, 122
Douglas Beekman 21, 80, 96, 106, 144
Harry Bennett 30
John Berkey 59, 104, 105, 110, 111, 115
Chris Blumrich 56, 57, 128
Don Brautigam 42, 106, 138, 144
John Butterfield 126, 144
Peter Caras 36, 46, 144
Alan E. Cober 76, 144
Mark Corcoran 20, 144
José Cruz 24
Vincent Di Fate 26, 47, 66, 106, 107, 113
Abe Echevarria 20, 81, 130
Dean Ellis 71, 114, 124, 125
Ray Feibush 24, 25
Stanislaw Fernandes 42, 48, 60, 112, 117
John Gampert 17, 94
Robert Giusti 137, 144
Robert Grossman 140, 141
Michael Herring 17, 88, 89
Steve Hickman 22, 40, 80, 90, 91, 102, 133, 136, 138
The Brothers Hildebrandt 34, 35, 144
Brad Holland 17, 20, 36, 74
Mark Ianacone 62
David McCall Johnston 82, 112
Ken Kelly 98
Vernon Kramer 17, 112, 136, 144
Larry Kresek 54, 55, 58, 75
Paul Lehr 39, 109, 116, 118, 119, 139
Robert Lo Grippo 62, 86, 87, 94
Carl Lundgren 17, 92
Wilson McLean 28, 70, 78, 79
Alan Magee 50, 66, 72, 88
Don Maitz 27, 44, 45, 99, 132, 136
Rick Meyerowitz 140
Ron Miller 126, 127
Charles Moll 50, 51, 102, 131
Jacqui Morgan 52, 70, 76

INDEX